SPEED to the REEF

BY KIM THOMPSON

ILLUSTRATED BY BRETT CURZON

A Little Honey Book

Crabtree Publishing

crabtreebooks.com

Introduction

This decodable story supports children as they:

1. Learn to read the high-frequency words shown below.

2. Learn to discriminate between the **short e** sound heard in *ref* and the **long e** sound heard in *reef*.

3. Learn to read words in which the **long e** sound has the spelling pattern **ee**.

Use the resources here to review sounds, letters, and words with young readers. Then, help them find and read the **long e** words in the story. Find more learning resources beginning on page 22. Happy reading!

High-Frequency Words

a	it	they
are	no	this
at	now	time
for	play	to
he	says	two
in	she	what
is	the	will

Sounds and Letters

The letters **e** and **e** form a vowel team. The **ee** team makes the **long e** sound. It sounds like the letter **e** saying its name.

Look at these words. The word *ref* has the **short e** sound you know. The word *reef* has the **long e** sound.

ref

reef

Read. Make the **long e** sound when you see **ee**.

eel

weed

green

teeth

3

Peek in the deep.

It is time for a meet.

4

Time to speed to the reef!

The ref checks the sheet.

The speeders are set.

The speeders are sleek.

"Now!" the ref says.

This is no time to freeze!

7

Sixteen gets a sneeze.

She seems green.

Time for bed.

Feel better, Sixteen!

Eel peeks.

Peeks between weeds.

Will Seventeen play?

He agrees!

Three are left.

A reel gets Fifteen.

He needs help.

Free Fifteen!

Two are left.

They see the reef!

Two keep speeding.

The end is steep!

Fourteen? Eighteen?

They are cheek to cheek.

Now Fourteen sweeps in.

She yells in glee!

Speeders say cheese.

They greet. They feed.

It is time to rest.

They will sleep for a week!

What is this at the reef?

It is TEETH!

NOW is the time for speed.

FLEE!

I Can Read!

Read **short e** words from the story.

bed	gets	rest
better	help	set
checks	left	yells
end	ref	

Read **long e** words from the story.

agrees	flee	peek	sneeze
between	fourteen	reef	speed
cheek	free	reel	speeders
cheese	freeze	see	speeding
deep	glee	seems	steep
eel	green	seventeen	sweeps
eighteen	greet	sheet	teeth
feed	keep	sixteen	three
feel	meet	sleek	weeds
fifteen	needs	sleep	week

Read sentences with **long e** words.

She needs sheets to sleep.

See the sleek green eel.

They need this cheese.

I Can Write!

Write each word on a piece of paper. Add **ee** in the blank. What words did you make? Use them to write sentences or stories.

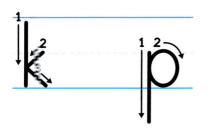

I Can Think!

1. What happens to racer 17?

2. Where does the race end? What is a reef?

3. Read the secret words. Find their pictures in the story.

feet   **knee**   **wheel**

Written by: Kim Thompson
Illustrated by: Brett Curzon
Designed by: Rhea Magaro
Series Development: James Earley
Educational Consultant: Marie Lemke M.Ed.

Crabtree Publishing

crabtreebooks.com   800-387-7650
Copyright © 2024 Crabtree Publishing

Printed in the U.S.A.
112023/PP20230920

Published in Canada
Crabtree Publishing
616 Welland Ave.
St. Catharines, Ontario
L2M 5V6

Published in the United States
Crabtree Publishing
347 Fifth Ave
Suite 1402-145
New York, NY 10016

Library and Archives Canada Cataloguing in Publication
Available at Library and Archives Canada

Library of Congress Cataloging-in-Publication Data
Available at the Library of Congress

Hardcover: 978-1-0398-3588-7
Paperback: 978-1-0398-3831-6
Ebook (pdf): 978-1-0398-3598-6
Epub: 978-1-0398-3608-2
Read-Along: 978-1-0398-3618-1
Audio: 978-1-0398-3628-0